The Cat who lost his Purr

Michele Coxon

Blackie
London

Bedrick/Blackie
New York

Bootle woke one morning without his purr.

His house was quiet and empty.
'Where is my purr?' wondered Bootle, who was normally happy and contented.
He washed and thought hard.
'When did I have it last?'
But like all cats he was not very good at remembering yesterday.

He didn't know about things like 'tomorrow', or the names of the days of the week.

Or even that the world was round. To him it was flat, and today it was purrless.

The things he knew were useful, like if it was a wet fur day or a dry fur day.

Or what time his tins were opened and when his milk was poured.

'I will go and find my purr,' decided Bootle and he set off.

Bootle started by looking in the bathroom.

Drip, drip, drip, drop, went the tap.

'Is this my purr?'

No, the wet drip sound was not his purr.

'Is my purr down here?'

No, it was not in the place where his unfurry friends sometimes sat.

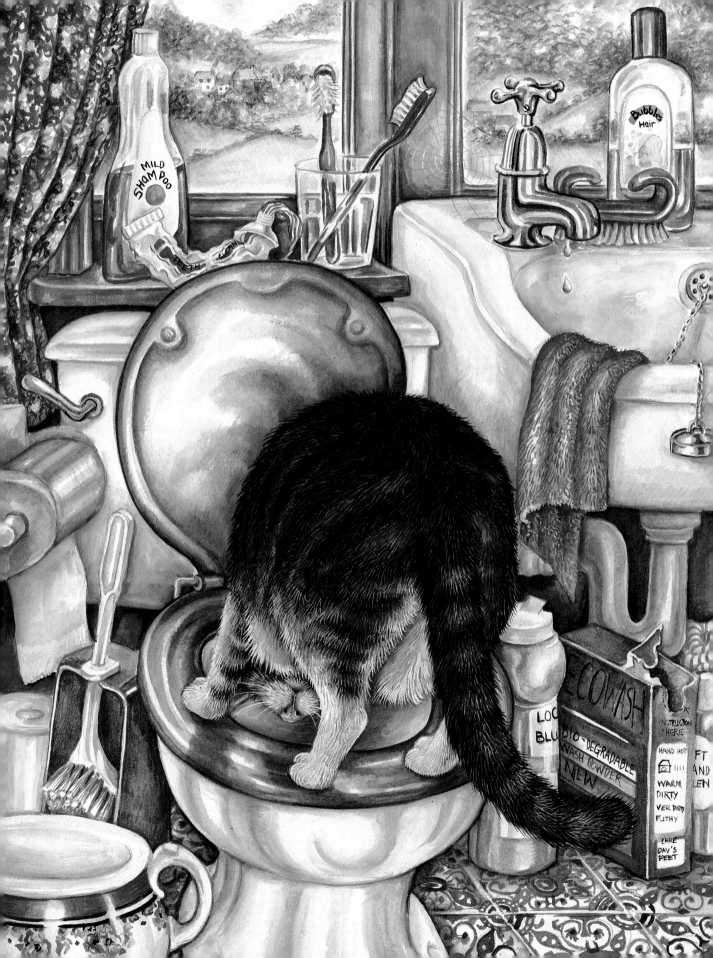

Bootle heard a sound very like his purr.
Buzz, buzz, buzz.
'Is this my purr?'
No, it was just a fly, so he ate it.
'Where did the noise go?' wondered
Bootle, licking his lips.

He went downstairs to the kitchen where there were lots of interesting sounds.

Humm, humm, humm.

The fridge hummed softly and it smelt good. Bootle was a clever cat, he knew how to open the fridge and look inside.

'Is my purr here?'

'No, not even inside the sausages' thought Bootle, feeling rather full.

There was a sound from under the cupboard.
Scratch, scratch, scratch, squeak.
'That sound could be my purr.'
But the scratch, squeak ran away from his fine, sharp claws.

A pleasant *Tick, tick, tock*, came
from the clock.
'Could that be my purr?' he wondered.
Bootle climbed up but a yellow bird
knocked him down with a loud
'Cuckoo!'
'Meow!' yelled Bootle.

In the laundry room the washing
monster made lots of loud, wet
gurgling noises.
Swish, swish, swash.
'Is my purr having a wash?'
Bootle thought a cat thought (which
isn't very long) and looked until his
whiskers felt dizzy.
'No, my purr is not there. It hates
getting wet.'

In the sitting room the fish blew bubbles
at him from their watery world.
Bubble, bubble, bubble.
Bootle didn't like getting his paws wet
either so he could not find out if the fish
had his purr. He turned away sadly.

'My purr must be outside in the sunshine. It loves the warm sun,' thought Bootle. But he had to chase away some naughty blue tits who were stealing his milk. *Crash!*

A thrush looked as if it might be
banging his poor purr on a stone.
Crack, crack, crack.
Bootle rushed to the rescue. But it was
only an unhappy snail which crawled
away without saying thank you.
Cats appreciate good manners.
Snails are always miserable and
never smile.

Bootle went back to the house in a down-tail mood.

Cats don't cry because that makes them wet.

'Poor me,' sighed Bootle.

He had a drink of milk, to help him think, and licked all the chocolate off some biscuits just for comfort.

And then he heard a sound. Lots of sounds, coming into the house.
Voices of his two-legged unfurry friends.
'My openers of cans.'
'My pourers of cream.'
'My strokers of fur.'
They were home and they had found his purr.
He purred with joy.
Purr, purr, purr, purr, purr.

At last his life (which to a cat means today) was purr-fect.

He was the most contented cat in the whole flat garden of his world and would be until the end of his whiskers.

And now his tale is told.

In memory of Karen and her husband Charlie and their children,
Ben, Katy and Becky.

Copyright © 1991 Michele Coxon
First published 1991 by Blackie Children's Books
This edition first published 1992

A CIP catalogue record for this book is available from the
British Library.

ISBN 0-216-93051-0

BLACKIE CHILDREN'S BOOKS
Penguin Books, Harmondsworth, Middlesex,
England, Australia, Canada, New Zealand

First American edition published in 1991 by
Peter Bedrick Books
2112 Broadway
New York, NY 10023
This edition first published 1992

Library of Congress Cataloging-in-Publication Data
Coxon, Michele
The cat who lost his purr/Michele Coxon.
– 1st American ed.
Summary: Bootle the cat searches inside and outside for his
lost purr and only retrieves it when his owners return.
ISBN 0-87226-453-X
[1. Cats–Fiction.]   I. Title
PZ7.C83945Cat   1991
[E]–dc20   90-14412   CIP   AC

Designed by Peggy Sadler
Printed in Hong Kong